This edition published by Parragon Books Ltd in 2014 and distributed by

Parragon Inc.
440 Park Avenue South, 13th Floor
New York, NY 10016
www.parragon.com

Written by Margaret Wise Brown   Illustrated by Emma Levey
Edited by Grace Harvey   Designed by Rachael Fisher
Production by Emma Fulleylove

ISBN 978-1-4723-6717-4

Printed in China

One More Rabbit ...

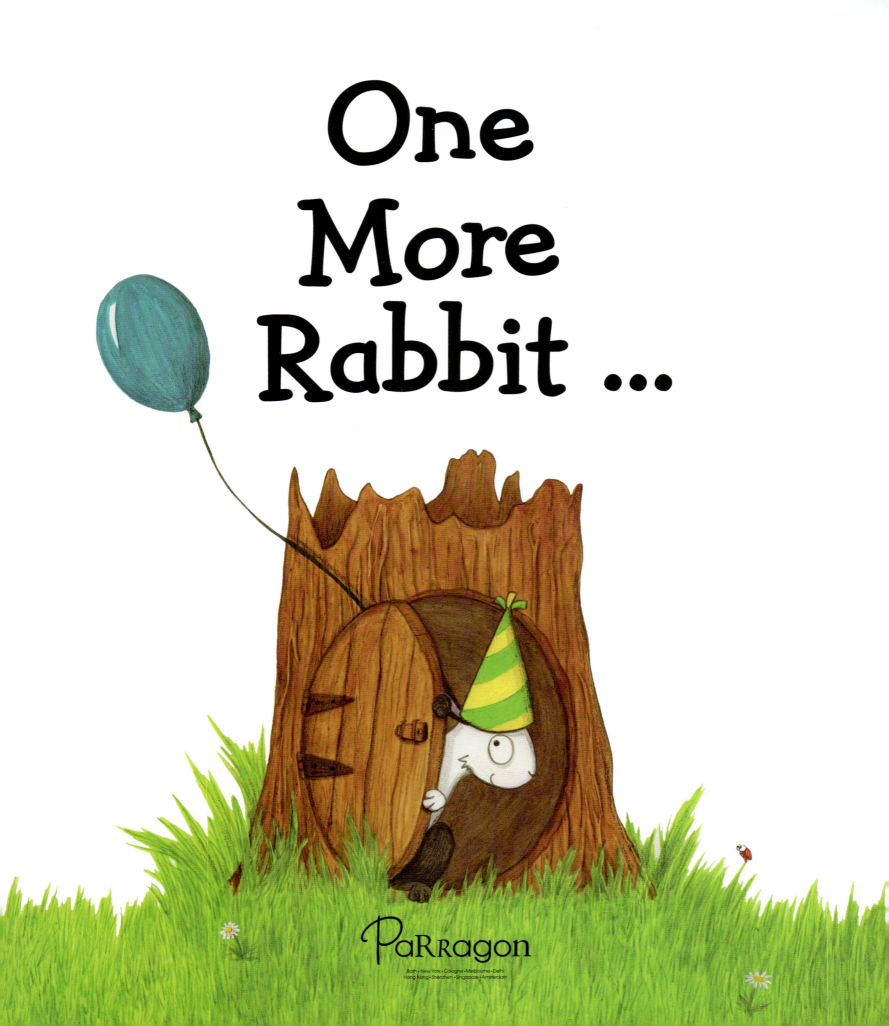

PaRragon

Bath • New York • Cologne • Melbourne • Delhi
Hong Kong • Shenzhen • Singapore • Amsterdam

Once upon a time, in a hollow tree stump, lived **one** excited rabbit with ...

HAPPY BIRTHDAY

one loving mother and ...

one loving father and ...

two

helpful sisters and ...

three

not-so-helpful brothers and ...

four
music-loving
uncles and ...

five

busy aunts and ...

six
troublemaking
cousins and ...

seven

impatient second cousins and ...

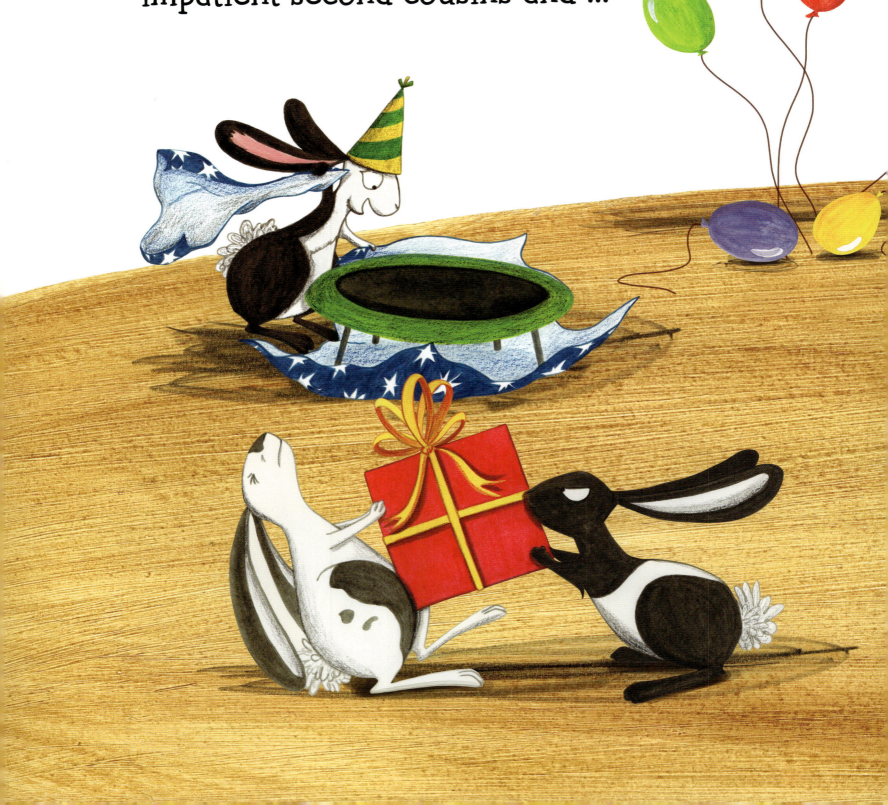

eight

merry third cousins and ...

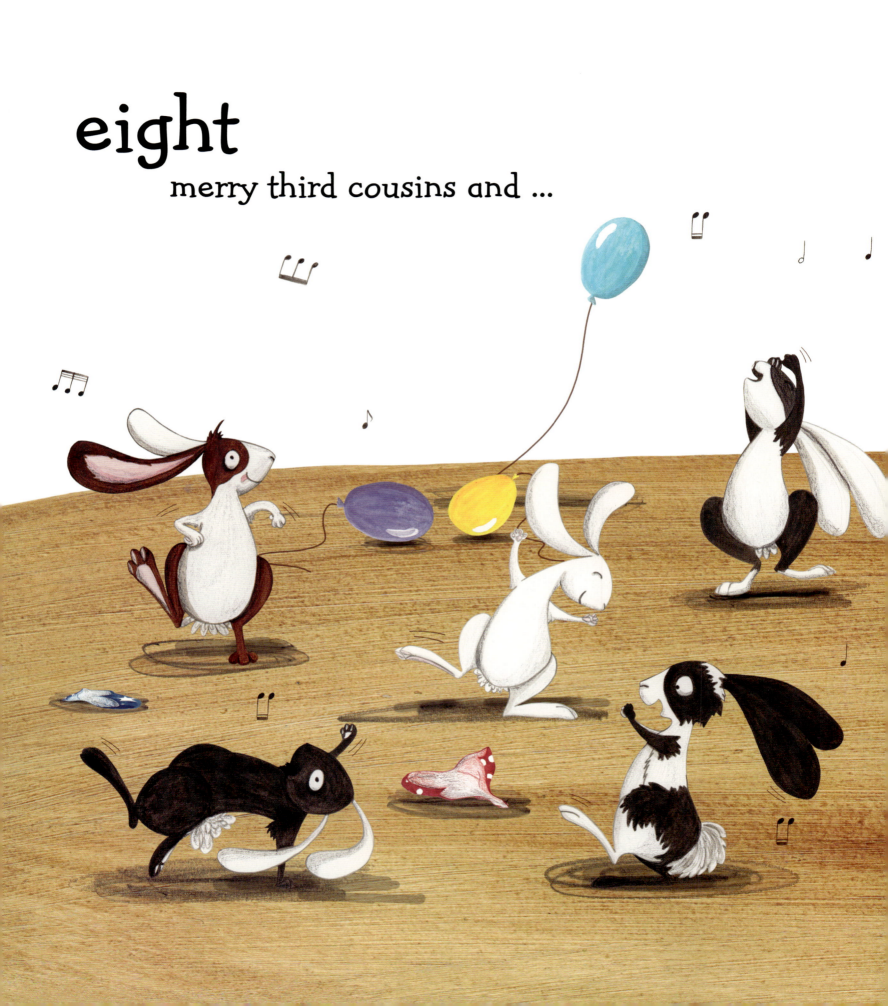

two

grooving grandmothers and ...

two

grooving grandfathers and ...

four talented great grandmothers and ...

four talented great grandfathers and ...

eight

toe-tapping great great grandmothers and ...

eight

toe-tapping great great
grandfathers and ...

one
delicious
birthday
carrot cake.
It didn't
last long ...

They were a BIG, warm rabbit family,
all in one clump.

And they all celebrated together
in a hollow tree stump ...

with a little excited rabbit
who was learning how to jump!